Dream Big

Believe,

& Enjoy the journey !

love

Kat Michaels

To the angels who have inspired me, to my mother Mary who has taught me the power of a smile, to my girls Danie, Lisa and Alyssa, to little Evan my miracle in disguise and most of all to my husband Michael who is living proof that happily ever after does exist.

A special thanks goes to Peter Parente and Tree of Life Publishing for their belief, support and ability to make a dream come true.

Tree of Life Publishing
1001 Avenue of the Americas
12th Floor
New York, NY 10018

Published by Tree of Life Publishing 2006.

Printed in Hong Kong.

Library of Congress Control Number: 2005910637

ISBN 0974505269

Willow's Bend

by Kat Michaels

Illustrated by Mike Motz

Down by the pond where the willow tree grows sat a little green frog with four little toes.
On a lily pad that was floating by, the frog looked for his breakfast, a big fat fly.

When all of a sudden from behind the old tree peeked
a chubby spry elf saying, "Come play with me."

The frog just croaked, "No, I'm a frog, you're an elf.
You'll just have to stay there and play by yourself, for
I am to busy looking for flies."
Then the sad elf looked up with tears in his eyes.
"I thought that maybe we could have fun."
"Oh no," croaked the frog as he soaked up the sun.
"We are too different to play on this day,"
and the sad little elf just walked away.

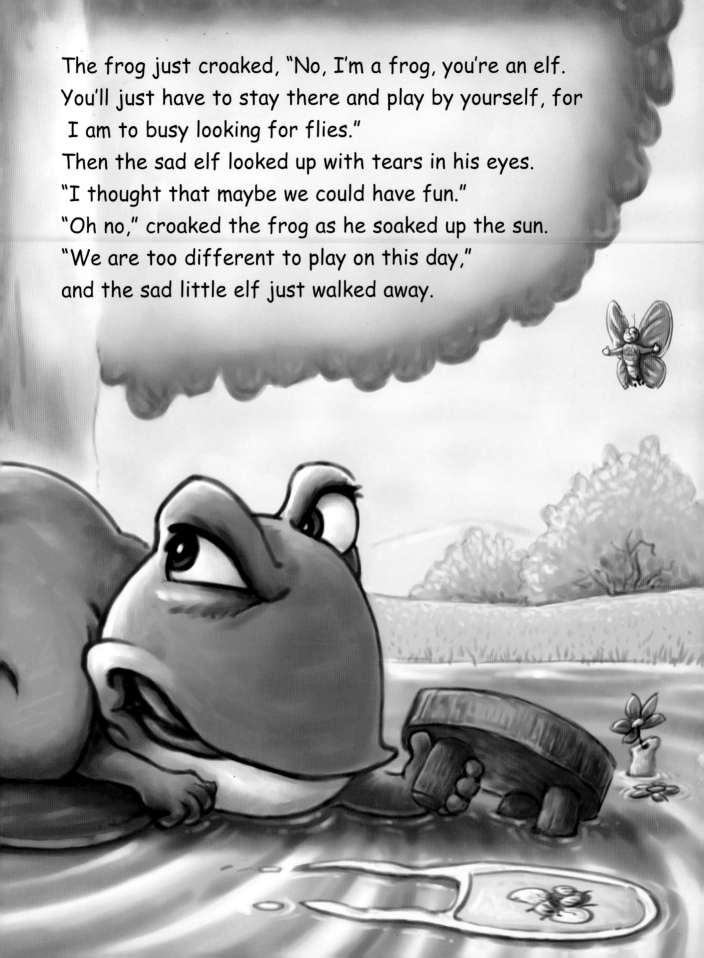

Then along came a butterfly bright as could be.
"Come on little frog will you play with me?"

"Oh no," said the frog, "that just won't do
for I can only hop, not fly like you."

So the pretty butterfly fluttered away
sad that the frog did not want to play.

Next came a rabbit who stopped for a drink.
He looked at the frog and said, "What do you think?"

"Would you like to come and play with me?
We could both jump high by the old willow tree."

The frog just croaked, "No", and the rabbit hopped away and the frog sat alone for the rest of the day.

Later that day another frog came by to sing a night song to the moon lit sky.

The little green frog said, "Come sit with me."

"I'd like to," said the frog, "but I'm going to the tree. That's where my friends are beneath the night sky, the elf, the rabbit and the pretty butterfly."

"We may be different but we are all friends and that's all that matters when the day ends."
Then the frog hopped on by heading back to the tree and then smiled and said, "You can come with me."

So the frogs hopped together to where the willow tree bends.

At the end of the day....It's nice to have friends.